Anonymous

More Echoes from the Oxford Magazine

being a second series of reprints of seven years

Anonymous

More Echoes from the Oxford Magazine
being a second series of reprints of seven years

ISBN/EAN: 9783337251109

Printed in Europe, USA, Canada, Australia, Japan

Cover: Foto ©Andreas Hilbeck / pixelio.de

More available books at **www.hansebooks.com**

MORE ECHOES

FROM

THE OXFORD MAGAZINE

Oxford
HORACE HART, PRINTER TO THE UNIVERSITY

MORE ECHOES

FROM THE

OXFORD MAGAZINE

BEING

A SECOND SERIES

OF

REPRINTS OF SEVEN YEARS

Oxford: 116 High Street

LONDON: HENRY FROWDE, AMEN CORNER, E.C.

1896

The Poems in this volume have been selected from those which have appeared in the OXFORD MAGAZINE between November, 1889, and November, 1896. Six of the poems by A. G. (pp. 21, 25, 30, 81, 83, 102), contributed originally to this journal, were reprinted in a volume, entitled "VERSES TO ORDER"; and are published again here under arrangement with Messrs. Methuen & Co.

The following signatures may be interpreted :—

D. F. A. . D. F. ALDERSON, *Magdalen College.*

R. L. B. . R. L. BINYON, *Trinity College.*

B. . . . C. E. BROWNRIGG, *Magdalen College.*

A. G. B. . A. G. BUTLER, *Oriel College.*

C. S. A. . A. S. CRIPPS, *Trinity College.*

W. J. F. . W. J. FERRAR, *Keble College.*

A. G. . . A. D. GODLEY, *Magdalen College.*

S. T. . . H. W. GREENE, *Magdalen College.*

D. G. H. . D. G. HOGARTH, *Magdalen College.*

W. P. K. . W. P. KER, *All Souls College.*

W. W. M. W. W. MERRY, *Lincoln College.*

H. A. M. . H. A. MORRAH, *St. John's College.*

J. S. P. . J. S. PHILLIMORE, *Christ Church.*

Q. . . . A. T. QUILLER-COUCH, *Trinity College.*

J. O'R. . J. O'REGAN, *Balliol College.*

Σ. . . . A. SIDGWICK, *Corpus Christi College.*

J. F. W. . J. FISCHER WILLIAMS, *New College.*

CONTENTS

—••—

Once, my dear—but the world was young
   then—
Magdalen elms and Trinity limes—
Lissom the oars and backs that swung then,
   Eight good men in the good old times—
Careless we, and the chorus flung then,
     Under St. Mary's chimes !

Reins lay loose and the ways led random—
   Christ Church meadow and Iffley track—
"Idleness horrid and dogcart" (tandem)—
   Aylesbury grind and Bicester pack—
Pleasant our lines, and, faith! we scanned
   'em :
     —Having that artless knack.

Come, old limmer, the times grow colder :
   Leaves of the creeper redden and fall.
Was it a hand, then, clapped my shoulder?
   —Only the wind by the chapel wall.
Dead leaves drift on thy lute : so — fold
   her
     Under thy faded shawl.

Never we wince though none deplore
  us,
  We who go reaping that we sowed;
Cities at cock-crow wake before us—
  Hey, for the lilt of the London road!
One look back, and a rousing chorus!
    Never a palinode!

Still on her spire the pigeons hover;
  Still by her gateway haunts the gown;
Ah, but her secret? You, young lover,
  Drumming her old ones forth from
    town,
Know you the secret none discover?
    Tell it—when *you* go down.

Yet if at length you seek her, prove her,
  Lean to her whispers never so nigh;
Yet if at last not less her lover
  You in your hansom leave the High;
Down from her towers a ray shall hover—
    Touch you, a passer-by!
              Q.

MUSA VENALIS

WHO will employ a doggrel bard?
    Come buy, come buy, come buy!
Butter and poetry sold by the yard,
    Come buy, come buy, come buy!
Don and tradesman, scholar and scout,
    Coach, smug, blood, professor and tout,
All will be suited without any doubt;
    Come buy, come buy, come buy!

I can praise your books, or perhaps your looks,
    And crack up your Licensed Halls;
I can chant every wicket you scattered at cricket
    With those terrible back-break balls;
Or your tiny boots and your stylish suits,
    Or how you got your Blue,
With your great flat back and your long thin legs,
    And the way you pulled it through.

B

Here is the shop for forging rhyme
   All in the latest modes,
Puffs supplied at a guinea a time,
   And Epinikian Odes.
I'll prattle of sheep, and how hills are steep,
   And roads are sometimes long,
Or lull you to slumbers with mystical numbers
   Of sweet Swinburnian song.
Epic, heroic, lyric or blank,
   Nothing to me comes hard,·
For I am a bard at a penny a line,
   A Quadrantarian Bard !

                                    J. O'R.

MVTAT TERRA VICES

Michaelmas Term, 1894.

'TIS Term again—once more the studious boy
Salutes his Dean with simulated joy:
Th' aspiring Fresher, with impartial view,
Reveres the Don, the Porter, and the Blue;
While Senior men to some admiring throng
Recount th' achievements of the recent Long,
And rusty students late from books remote
Read the dark text and con the obscurer note.
Golfers resume their caddies and their clubs,
Greats men their Plato, History men their Stubbs;
Perspiring oarsmen ply the straining oar,
And Learning smiles upon her sons once more!
Yet ah! what sadness mars the festive scene?
Why stalk the Proctors with dejected mien?
Why falters History at the name of BOYD,
Sheds a still tear, and mourns an aching void?

Change rules the world : and e'en a VICE'S power
Is but the creature of a fleeting hour.
His state neglected and his pomp forgot
(What boots his Bedel, and his Poker what ?)
In Sheldon's Theatre no more will he
Calm the wild throng and grant the high degree :
No more control the tedious dull debates
Of Boards (himself more bored) and Delegates :
Post-prandial sermons soothe his ears no more :
Our Term begins, but his, alas! is o'er!

   My pensive Muse! attempt a lighter strain ;
Be more hilarious, and begin again.
As fields grow green that erst were bare and
      brown ;
As men come up, though other men go down ;
As new-born flowrets deck the vernal meads ;
As Amurath to Amurath succeeds—
Nature benign her losses quick restores,
And grants us still her new Vice-Chancellors!
What rays of light illume our darkest scenes,
And gild with joy the pepper-box of Queen's?
We hail the radiance of thy nascent star,
VIR INSIGNISSIME, J. R. MAGRATH!

A. G.

AD LECTIONEM SUAM

WHEN Autumn's winds denude the grove,
    I seek my Lecture, where it lurks
'Mid the unpublished portion of
    My works,

And ponder, while its sheets I scan,
    How many years away have slipt
Since first I penned that ancient man-
    -uscript.

I know thee well—nor can mistake
    The old accustomed pencil stroke
Denoting where I mostly make
    A joke,—

Or where coy brackets signify
    Those echoes faint of ancient wit
Which, if a lady's present, I
    Omit.

Though Truth enlarge her widening range,
   • And Knowledge be with time increased,
While thou, my Lecture! dost not change
    The least,

But fixed immutable amidst
    The advent of a newer lore,
Maintainest calmly what thou didst
    Before :

Though still malignity avows
    That unsuccessful candidates
To thee ascribe their frequent ploughs
    In Greats—

Once more for intellectual food
    Thou 'lt serve : an added phrase or two
Will make thee really just as good
    As new :

And listening crowds, that throng the spot,
    True Learning's cup intent to drain,
Will cry, " The old familiar rot
    Again ! "

A. G.

OUR MASTERS: AN ECLOGUE

*The endowment of Research is an old story: the endowment of the
Extension Lectures is a modern demand and backed by a louder
outcry. The resources of the University are insufficient for the
needs of liberal studies; but this is no answer, as is shown in the
following dialogue, to the rapacity of the specialist and the sciolist.*

RESEARCHER.

I AM not such as others are;
My worth is hard to rate,
And you must please to take at par
My modest estimate.
For how can you examine those
Who only know what none else knows?
Or—if you choose to put it so—
What no one else would care to know?
`

EXTENSION STUDENT.

I'm very much as others are,
Perhaps a little more so.
I don't pursue my studies far,
For then I find they bore so.

By each successive teacher shown
Glimpses half-seen of things half-known,
I represent, throughout the land,
The second-rate at second-hand.

RESEARCHER.

My learning's tree bears scanty fruits,
  For I'm a true Researcher;
I find in Letto-Slavic roots
  My intellectual nurture.
      Of these I know, and I alone,
      The little that can e'er be known;
      Content therewith I stand apart
      From science, literature, and art.

EXTENSION STUDENT.

I pass all knowledge in review,
  The subjects don't much matter;
I pick up quite enough to do
  For dinner-table chatter.
      A note-book, large and full, contains
      My substitutes for work and brains:
      And I believe with all my soul
      "The half is greater than the whole."

ENSEMBLE.

In this at least we both concur,
  We somehow must be paid for;
Curators of the Chest demur,
  But *we* are what they're made for.
    Of Letters, once esteemed Humane,
    The day has sunk, nor dawns again—
    Quick then—endow us, for you must,
    Extensionist and Dryasdust.

X. Y. Z.

BLUES

WHEN the bard selects a subject which is suitable
    to sing,
'Tisn't Love, or Convocation, but it's quite another
    thing—
For the monumental records of elevens and of
    crews
Are the only theme that's proper for the academic
    Muse:
      'Tis the sinews and the thews
      And the victories of Blues:
They're the solitary subject which is likely to
    amuse—
Yes, the only dissertations that the public will
    peruse
Are the chronicles relating the performances of
    Blues.

When I move in gilded circles ('tis my habit now
    and then),
I am voted dull and stupid, and I am not asked
    again,

If I cannot make a series of intelligent remarks
In replying to their queries on the River and the
    Parks,
    Where they gather in a swarm
    When it's reasonably warm,
And they watch the Blue at cricket and they
    prattle of his Form,
Where they see him a-compiling of a century or two,
Or applaud him from the Barges as he sits among
    his crew.

When I read my weekly *Isis* (as I usually do),
I peruse with veneration the achievements of the
    Blue :
Where his catalogue of virtues is hebdomadally
    penned
By the callow admiration of a sympathetic friend :
    He's the idol every week
    Of a sympathetic clique
For his prowess on the River or his ignorance of
    Greek ;
And the Freshman, while the record he assiduously
    cons,
Sees a model and ensample for the guidance of
    his Dons !

In those old monastic cloisters where the learned
    meet to dine
He's the theme of envious Tutors while they sit
    beside their wine:
They neglect their ancient studies, and the books
    upon their shelves
Are the latest works on cricket—which they do
    not play themselves.
      Yes! the Don no more dilates
      On the facts and on the dates
Which will benefit his pupils when he sends them
    in for Greats;
For the columns of the *Sportsman* are the only
    thing he knows,
And he sets them to his scholars as a piece for
    Latin Prose.

Ye magnificent young athletes! whom we contem-
    plate with awe,
Whose behaviour is our model and whose wishes
    are our law—
Who to honour your successes burn our chairs and
    tables, while
E'en the owner acquiesces with a simulated smile,

Simply asking now and then
If you're ordinary men,
Or phenomena celestial who are granted to our
ken:
Take this humble little lay
From a reverent M.A.
As the only act of homage he is competent to
pay—
For the truth's as old as Pindar, that the only thing
to do
Is to court the approbation and indulgence of a
Blue!

·A. G.

TERMINALIA

SALVE Termine summe Terminorum
infinitaque Termini voluptas!
salvete, hospitium recens, sorores,
consobrinae, amitaeque,—ceteraeque.
consobrina placet domi forisque:
dulces, si modo mutuae, sorores:
placandasque amitas, puer, memento,
si vis conloquio frui puellae.

Aestas praeterit, imminetque Finis:
i nunc, Subgraduate, pelle curas:
Horti, Commemoratio, Choreae,
Ludi, Prandia, Remigationes,—
quid non laetitiae reducit hora?
gaude, Subgraduate, nil agendo.

Matutinus abi; require Pratum—
laburni loca pendulo monili
et ranunculeo nitentia auro,
Maio castaneisque odora conis—
vestes exue: recreare fluctu:
dulces Isideae lavationes.

collegi citius redi Penates:
explorator adest: cibus paratur:
bullit Mochius humor: ova, salmo,
panis, cuncta vocant: eas, sodales
expergefacias inertiores.
dulces ante meridiem induenti
navalis toga candidaeque braccae,—
braccae finibus infimis retortae.
lecturasque secare dulce: dulces
post ientacula fumigationes.
Tutores vacua querantur aula:
Praeses dilaceret comas, genusque
inritabile saeviant Decani:
nullius miserere: temne libros:
per quadrangula lentus ambulato,
libans Acta Diurna seu Rubentem,
cari non sine fistula vaporis.
cum Phoebi medius peractus ardor,
conto linter eat per Interamna;
dum sudant alii, iace supinus,
fuma, perlege Gallicam novellam:
aut tu rete super pilam remittas,
aut spectaveris Undecim virorum
plagas, Antipodesque praeliantes.
quinta est hora, redi, revise amicos;

fumant Serica pocla: carpe fessus
plusquamsardanapaleam quietem.
tum convivia, musicique coetus,
serae vesperis ambulationes,
ludi, charta, ioci, fragor, theatrum,
Campani latices, vel unda Oporti,
seu quem mitigat Usquebacchianum
aut Sodae liquor aut Apollinaris;—
dulce est desipere in loco studentis,
praetextuque laboris otiari.

Salve Termine summe Terminorum,
O conferte gravisque inanitate,
O dulcedine perlaboriose,
Saturnalia dissipationis!

Σ.

MURRAY'S HANDBOOK TO HOMER

"*We regretted much to see* PROFESSOR MURRAY *of Glasgow lending
the weight of his brilliant name to the statement that schoolboys
ought not to read Homer, because it would corrupt their Greek.*"
—Note in the OXFORD MAGAZINE.

"*Poluphloisboisterous Homer of old
Threw all his augments into the sea,
Although he had often been courteously told
That perfect imperfects begin with an e:
But the poet replied with a dignified air
'What the Digamma does any one care?'*"

Yes—it is true that that singular man
(Whether he's Homer, or somebody else)
Often puts κεν where he should have put ἄν,
Seldom will construe and mostly misspells,
And wholly ignores those grand old laws
Which govern the Attic conditional clause.

This is the author whom innocent boys
Cram for Responsions and grind at for Mods,
Possible Ithacas, mythical Troys,
Scandalous stories of heroes and gods,

C

Wholly deficient in morals and truth,—
That is the way that we educate Youth!

Even the great Alexandrian clique
  Never attempted to write him anew:
Great Mr. Murray, Professor of Greek!
  Erudite person! they left it to you.
Now shall we have—'twas a manifest need—
Something that serious scholars can read.

Parents and guardians may surely expect
  Books where the student orthography learns,
Language grammatical, spelling correct,
  Not the vagaries of Chaucer or Burns,—
Syntax and idioms adapted to those
Stated distinctly in Sidgw-ck's Greek Prose:

None of the puzzles that puzzle us now,
  Nothing to hinder disciple or don,
All of his genitives ending in ου,
  All of his ἅπαξ λεγόμενα gone—
Homer conforming to classical rule—
That is the Homer for College and School!

A. G.

OF CHAUCERS ROSEMOUNDE

BALADE TO THE MAKERES

MAISTRES that in the goodly sees divyne
the brighte Apolo with the laurer crounde,
we thanken yow that of youre hye ingyne
on erthe yit the crommes ben yfounde:
loo Aristotle in Egipte under grounde
that of Athenes wroot the governaunce,
and Chaucer thy balade of Rosemounde
of joye encresing oure inheritaunce.

Youre loos schal nat apairen ne decline:
sendeth us more of that wherin ye habounde
(ne yit of Melibee the discipline
reherseth nat for hit nis nat jocounde)
loo with oblivioun was longe ywounde
Granson the flour of hem that maken in Fraunce,
and now he is unwrien and al unbounde,
of joye encresing oure inheritaunce.

C 2

Thogh Troye be toscatered in ruine,
and Thebes brent, and Ninive forgrounde,
yit nis ther comen among us swiche a pine
to jompre the olde musyk ne confounde
the swete layes, ne the voys facounde,
ne putte here mirthe oute of oure remembraunce:
the Hous of Fame endureth yit a stounde,
of joye encresing our inheritaunce.

L'Envoy.

Goth, litel lewede rimes cercling rounde,
loketh ye be nat blamed of bobaunce
ther sotil lore is and the craft profounde,
of joye encresing our inheritaunce.

W. P. K.

Kal. Mai, 1891.

PROCTORS IN PROCESSION

The Proctors asserted their right to precede M.A. Heads of Houses.

QUI contemptu pressus est, ecce fit sublimis,
quique summus fuerat mixtus est cum imis :
anne vos iniurias perferetis tales,
Guardiani, Praesides, atque Principales ?

olim in Ecclesiam Universitatis
praecedebant maximae viri dignitatis :
ibant cum Doctoribus Capita Domorum
in Doctorum cathedras, sicut est decorum :

primus venit omnium Bromi de sacello
Vice Cancellarius, ductus a bedello :
Procurator pone tum, Praeses ibat ante
(tintinnabulario rite tintinnante).

ordo nunc euntium notus exolescit,
deprimuntur Capita, Procurator crescit,
nunc (velut petorritis si trahantur equi)
idem hic praegreditur qui solebat sequi !

Caput Domus quodlibet est permagnus homo,
nihil potest propria exturbare domo:
Procurator annua tantum habet iura,
utque vere dixerim, servus est natura.

alter fiet—nihil est quare metuatis—
unus e Collegio Universitatis:
neu collega terreat: brevi fiet iste
mera pars Collegii Divi Jo. Baptistae.

vivunt illi regulas persequendo stultas,
propter parva crimina imponendo multas:
sunt interdum utiles, verum plane pestis:
vos cum illis nulla re comparandi estis.

Sive vos in praelio trucidabit Freeman,
—sanguis certe Praesidum bonae legis semen,—
morte contumelias peius ferre tales,
Guardiani, Praesides, atque Principales!

A. G.

NONSENSE VERSES

After SWINBURNE, *Poems and Ballads*, i. 116.

IF I were what the year is,
   And you the Summer Term ;
Involved and yet unmated
We might be correlated
As pewter unto beer is,
   Or thrush to early worm :
If I were what the year is,
   And you the Summer Term.

If you were classic poet,
   And I the humble crib,
Apart—you 'd be neglected,
And I—not much respected ;
Plato without his Jowett,
   A pen without a nib :
If you were classic poet,
   And I the humble crib.

If you were a papyrus,
    And I a palimpsest,
We'd lurk, assorted oddly,
In nooks and holes of Bodley,
Where trippers can't admire us
    And students daren't molest :
If you were a papyrus,
    And I a palimpsest.

If you were the Vice-Chancellor,
    And I the poker bore ;
We'd wend our walks diurnal,
Half formal, half fraternal,
Like Gretel and like Hansel, or
    The Heavenly Twins of yore :
If you were the Vice-Chancellor,
    And I the poker bore.

If you re-wrote the Digest,
    And I revised the Code,
We'd frolic with opinions
That never were Justinian's,
And dance, with quip and high jest,
    Down learning's royal road :
If you re-wrote the Digest,
    And I revised the Code.

If I could be the whisky,
  And you the soda were,
'Mid shouts and glasses' jingle
We'd sparkle, mix and mingle,
With Undergraduates frisky,
  Nor here—nor quite all there :
If I could be the whisky,
  And you the soda were.

If you, love, were the bonfire,
  And I the College chairs,
In fire we'd seek sensation
Of mutual, glad cremation,
Fire, that seems sunk and gone—fire
  That faintlier—flickering—flares :
If you, love, were the bonfire,
  And I the College chairs.

                        X. Y. Z.

CAVENDISH: AN ODE

On the extinction of Cavendish College in the University of Cambridge.

I.

AND can it be? is Cambridge too
  To Ignorance a slave?
Can dark Reaction's tide imbrue
  The Cam's progressive wave?
I used to think that every fad,
That every scheme and purpose mad
  In Education's sphere,
A Kindergarten system, or
A theory of Mr. St—rr,
  Could find expansion here!

II.

As golfers, doomed by fortune harsh
To seek the flats of Cowley Marsh,
Still turn a wistful eye upon
The verdant slopes of Headington,
So Cavendish—a pigmy race—

Laments th' obnoxious rule
Which closes that peculiar place,
    The Cambridge Infant School.
How oft—when privileged to view
    Amid some rural scene
Her freshmen, walking two and two,
    Escorted by the Dean—
How oft her halls I seemed to see,
Where, dandled on the Master's knee,
    They learn their ὁ, ἡ, τό,
And little Pollmen lisp with glee
    About their Little-go !
Not there (I thought) the studious boy
Is taught to fill, with lawless joy,
    The gay nocturnal cup :
At half-past eight—or so 'tis said—
The Tutor sends his men to bed,
    And comes to tuck them up !
No "gates" or fines pollute the air :
No scholarships or prizes there
    Reward successful cram,
But Vice is spanked (though not too hard)
And Virtue finds its due reward
    In extra helps of jam.

III.

Such was the scene: but human bliss
   Is bound, alas! to pass away :
And Cavendish no longer is,
   Because she did not pay.
An exiled crew, her students wend—
   Their corals lost, their rattles broke—
For Cavendish has found an end
   (As usual) in smoke:
And once again on history's page
   Is chronicled the truth—
Youth cannot live with crabbed Age,
   Nor crabbed Age with Youth.

A. G.

LINES TO AN OLD FRIEND

WHEN we're daily called to arms by continual
   alarms,
And the journalist unceasingly dilates
On the agitating fact that we're soon to be
   attacked
By the Germans, or the Russians, or the States:
When the papers all are swelling with a patriotic
   rage,
And are hurling a defiance or a threat,
Then I cool my martial ardour with the pacifying
   page
Of the *Oxford University Gazette.*

When I hanker for a statement that is practical
   and dry
(Being sated with sensation in excess,
With the vespertinal rumour and the matutinal lie
Which adorn the lucubrations of the Press),

Then I turn me to the columns where there's
   nothing to attract,
 Or the interest to waken and to whet,
And I revel in a banquet of unmitigated fact
 In the *Oxford University Gazette.*

When the Laureate obedient to an editor's decree
 Puts his verses in the columns of the *Times*;
When the endless minor poet in an endless minor
   key
 Gives the public his unnecessary rhymes;
When you're weary of the poems which they
   constantly compose,
 And endeavour their existence to forget,
You may seek and find repose in the satisfying
   prose
 Of the *Oxford University Gazette.*

In that soporific journal you may stupefy the
   mind
 With the influence narcotic which it draws
From the Latest Information about Scholarships
   Combined
 Or the contemplated changes in a clause:

Place me somewhere that is far from the *Standard*
  and the *Star*,
From the fever and the literary fret,—
And the harassed spirit's balm be the academic
  calm
Of the *Oxford University Gazette!*

A. G.

A BOATING SONG

Now the winter's fairly gone,
    Come, my trusty crew,
Take your seats and paddle on:
    Touch her, bow and two!
Coach and College on you call:
    Now's the time to show
What you're made of: Forward all,
    Are you ready? Row!

Chorus.

    Row, row, row!
Swinging out and all together,
Steady, steady on the feather,
    Now then, make her go!
Even keel and blades as true,
Keep it long and pull it thro',
Buck up for the old Dark Blue,
    And row, row, row!

You who've gone to Putney's tide
    Heavy with our fate;
Try, as you have ever tried,
    Gallant Oxford Eight!
And, whatever may befall,
    Put in all you know,
When you hear the "Forward all,
    Are you ready? Go!"

    (Chorus, as before.)

DIALOGUS DE CONGREGATIONE TUTORIS ET MAGISTRI EXTRANEI

On a proposal to deprive resident Masters of Arts, not endowed by their Colleges, of their vote in Congregation.

Tutor.

ABI, vir extraneus, in longinquas aedes!
obscurantistariis hic est nulla sedes:
non hic suffragabere si monenti credes;
amovebo statim te, sponte ni concedes.

rerum quid intellegis academicarum?
crede, non peritus es quaestionum harum:
et, si causae ceterae suffecerunt parum,
habes in Oxonia curam animarum.

Magister Extraneus.

Parce, precor, clericis: namque tali de re
nihil est, quod videam, cur sic indignere:
atqui velim scire cur—si docebis vere—
nefas sit suffragium nobis exercere.

sunt quae non intellegam: verum est quod mones:
ubi tamen limites intellectus pones?
tune, cum Scientiae postulant ut dones,
technicas intellegis disputationes?

T.

Non est ius suffragii largiendum cuivis
(atque quam paucissimis e Conservativis):
si non in Collegio vel in Aula vivis
nunquam potes sapere ; tu es merus civis.

M. E.

Quod sis in Collegio si videtur satis,
sique nemo sapiens habitat in stratis,
cum vos in Collegiis soli non vivatis,
date suffragandi ius undergraduatis.

T.

Argumento breviter respondemus isti—
ego sum vir eminens, Tutor Aedis Christi :
tuque, quamquam talibus non est fas resisti,
semper hic suffragia contra me tulisti.

M. E.

Nihil curo quisnam sis : namque—plane fabor—
suffragatum veni huc, atque suffragabor.
si conaris pellere, vanus erit labor :
namque iusto munere nunquam deprivabor.

(*Explicit Dialogus et intrant in Domum Convoca-
tionis pugnantes.*)

A. G.

A STUDY IN PATIENCE

With apologies to MR. GILBERT.

IF you're anxious for to shine in the Philanthropic
    line, you should let yourself be seen
Entertaining of a Mission which has made an
    expedition from the wilds of Bethnal Green:
You should feel no idle scruples in postponing all
    your pupils, and in putting off the work they
    bring,
For to act as educator to the lower social strata
    is a much more noble thing—
    And all your guests will say, when you've
    tramped the livelong day,
"'E's one of them good-for-nothing lazy Dons,
    as 'as got no work to do,
So 'ow could 'e be better employed than chaperon-
    ing me and you?"

You will traverse all the tangles of your cloisters
    and quadrangles with a bored and blasé band,
You will indicate the Garden and the Chapel and
    the Warden with a vague discursive hand,

And your antiquarian knowledge while in every
   Hall and College you display with decent
   pride,
They will check your observations with an ill-
   concealed impatience and an *Alden's Oxford
   Guide.*
   And every one will say, while they slowly,
      sadly stray,
" This is all very well for uncultivated coves what
   'asn't been here before,
But a hintellectooal man like me—why, 'e pines
   for something more! "

When aweary of discourses you have marshalled
   out your forces, and conduct your errant
   charge
To the most convenient places for spectators of
   the races, on a raft, or bank, or barge,
Your remarks upon the crews—meant for instruction and amusement—with indifference blank
   they'll view,
Or will stigmatize as drivel (which is possibly
   uncivil, but is—broadly speaking—true).
   And the serious ones will say " Why! they
      don't do nought but play !

If this kind of thing is the end and aim of a
    Universitee,
They had better tike and confiscate the blooming
    place for the benefit of you and me!"

You will ask them (from an inner sense of recti-
    tude) to dinner, where your anxious soul
    you'll try
By attempting as you revel to assume a lower
    level and abstain from subjects high :
Condescension philanthropic will suggest the proper
    topic, and you'll think (delusion blind !)
That the questions you have mooted are particu-
    larly suited to the average Cockney mind.
  So every one will say, when at last they go
    away,
"That this young man is a hignorant chap it is
    perfectly plain to see,
For the 'Igher Heducation is the only thing as
    reely interests me!"

                      A. G.

A SCHOOL OF FLIRTATION

In the Eights Week, 1891, *when the now established Final School of English Literature had first been mooted seriously.*

ONCE more but in vain we resist her,
  Our colours come fluttering down
To the smile of the somebody's sister,
  To the eyes of the cousin from Town.
By courtesy lords of creation,
  We follow a scampering skirt,
And must still con the old conjugation
  "I flirted, I flirt, I shall flirt."

Is this then a time for the faddist
  To broach a new serious School,
While frivolity reigns at its maddest,
  When every one's playing the fool?
If he "aims at a real relation
  Of studies to schools," as he states,
Let him move for a School of Flirtation
  To be held in the week of the Eights!

For desks, give the candidates pillows,
　　Let punts take the place of the Schools,
Let *viva* be held under willows,
　　None near but the fish in the pools;
Let one give another suggestions,
　　And chaperones slumber the while,
And let the Examiner's questions
　　Be framed in the following style:

" If A be good-looking and 20:
　　If B be divine and 18:
If C be—well—50, with plenty
　　Of wits preternaturally keen:
Can you show by what use of quadratics
　　The squaring of C may be done?
And when by applied mathematics
　　Will 18 and 20 be 1?

" Express by the rule of proportion
　　The value of 'sisterly love,'
And state what amount of precaution
　　Is required to convert the above:
Work the sum out in full, then express it
　　In practice, and find the mistake:
Is there any known way to redress it?
　　And how many hearts will it break?"

What danger, with cousins for coaches,
  Of defeat or disgrace in this School?
What need of a tutor's reproaches
  To enforce such a monitor's rule?
With such guides it may safely be reckoned
  That even the idlest and worst
In a week would be sure of a second,
  In a fortnight could count on a first!

D. G. H.

THE METEOROLOGIST TO HIS
MISTRESS

HE.

WAVES of caloric that warm and refresh are
   Spreading benignly o'er mountain and plain:
Then—while an area of limited pressure
   Causes a local cessation of rain—
Haste to the river! where willows and sedges stir,
   Bowed by the breeze from the westering sun—
Zephyrs, whose force anemometers register
   Not in excess of 2·1!

SHE.

Study, O study the chart in the paper:
   Look at the glass and be guided by that!
What's a Solidified Stratum of Vapour?
   Doesn't it mean I shall ruin my hat?
Wet and despairing, the elements' gloom you'll eye,
   Doomed from the downpour to cower and to
      flinch,
Watching the nebulous cirri and cumuli
   Add to the rainfall by more than an inch.

HE.

Courage! nor deem that your Strephon's discretion
  Does not provide for potential mishaps :
E'en the approach of a Shallow Depression
  Nothing demands but umbrellas and wraps.
Come! and at ease in my shallop reclining
  There I will whisper an amorous tale,
While in the firmament cloudlessly shining
  Anticyclonic conditions prevail!

A. G.

ΔΑΚΡΥΟΕΝ ΓΕΛΑΣΑΣ

" Smiles that fade in tears."

ONCE more our visitors arrive by dozens,
           " They come," is still the cry:
Mothers and sisters and delightful cousins
           Parade the High.

In turn they fill the old familiar places,
           Smile sweet and whisper low ;
But some of us regret the vanished faces
           Loved long ago.

In honour of her eyes his latest ballad
           The poet touches up:
The host with care compounds the lobster salad,
           Or claret cup.

So through the golden weather youth rejoices:
           But those whose spring is past
Sit vainly listening for remembered voices
           Grown still at last.

At night with pretty Dorothy and Daisy
           The man who goes to balls,
Like Mr. Swiveller, essays "the mazy,"
           And sometimes falls.

For some such things have fled beyond recalling,
   Gone with the days that were;
They hear no dainty footstep lightly falling
   Upon the stair.

Flirtations, picnics, music, fêtes, and laughter,
   .With vows of endless truth,
A happy Now, a happier Hereafter,
   The dreams of youth—

These turn to silence, solitude, and sorrow,
   And thoughts of yesterday,
With those who look no longer for to-morrow,
   Whose heads are gray.

ENVOI.

Is this a jest or sober meditation?
   Faith, who can tell?   Not I,
Who know not whether this Commemoration
   To laugh or cry.

        S. T.

MEISTER WILHELM IN OXFORD

In February, 1890, Mr. GLADSTONE, of Christ Church and All Souls, came into residence. The following verses are republished with an apology to the shade of the " poor organist " who interviewed Master Hugues of Saxe-Gotha.

HIST! but a word; beg your pardon;
   Hear a poor Master of Arts
Eager to learn of the wisdom of Hawarden :
   What do you mean by this " Union of hearts "?
See, we're alone in the garden—

I, the poor lecturer here,
   You, sir, a statesman of note,
Trusted and followed this many a year :
   Let's have a colloquy, something to quote.
Mansfield will prick up its ear!

Here's your Bill, younger folks shelve :
   You dropped it so off-hand and runningly.
See, here's your masterpiece, clause number twelve :
   Why was it whisked into limbo so cunningly,
Hatchet sent after the helve?

Now you give nought but a phrase
   Nothing propound, that I see :

Parnell might blame it, or Salisbury praise,
  Guarded, no less, where no safeguard needs be,
Starting us all different ways.

Morley his aid interposes;
  Harcourt is eager to help;
Ripon and Rosebery thrust in their noses:
  So the cry's open, the kennel's a-yelp:
Childers confusedly proses.

Morley is dreadfully candid;
  Asquith discepts, has distinguished;
Harcourt votes solid, if ever yet man did;
  Freeman protests; says it isn't the thing wished:
Back to You comes the case bandied.

Parnell is curt and corrosive;
  Sexton grows nettled and crepitant;
Billy O'Brien's expansive, explosive;
  Tanner outdoes them all, strident and strepitant;
Davitt— O Danaids, O Sieve!

Now 'tis evictions and crowbars,
  Now 'tis a logical tissue
Fine as a web of the casuist Escobar's
  Worked on this bone of a bill—to what issue?
"Freedom," you cry—are there no bars?

I for your effort am zealous:
　Prove we were wrong when we doubted:
Seems it surprising a lover grows jealous,
　Hopes 'twas for something the caucuses shouted,
Cheering those Parnellite fellows?

Over our heads Truth and Nature
　Smile on these zigzags and dodges:
Ins and Outs—plans for a new Legislature,
　Is there a point where the sense of it lodges,
Safe from mere talk's usurpature?

My notion—I know that I'm right here
　. . . The gate, sir! he's going to lock it.
Hallo you, Simon, just show us a light here!
　Down dips his light like a rocket!
He's a Tory, old Simon: he'd like, unawares
To keep the place locked up till next morning
　prayers,
To find two Home Rulers had ended their cares
At the foot of these rotten old moss-moulded
　stairs:
　Have you got half-a-crown in your pocket?

T. R.

DER ALTMANN IN OXFORD

DER Altmann vent to Oxford,
  He drafel fast und far,
He rided shoost for sixdy miles
  All in von rail-roat car.
"I knows foost rate how far I'fe goed,
  I'fe gounted carefully,
Dere vas shoost von shbeech each vifdeen miles,"
  Said Altemann, said he.

Als bei de Reating bladform
  A shtop de Schnellzug makes,
Dere coomed a poy und offered him
  Soom Banburische cakes.
"I'fe svallowed all mein brincibles,
  Dot's nur ein Scherz for me,
Boot I ton't dink I can svallow dese,"
  Said Altemann, said he.

E

He vent to Chichele's College
  Ash dreimals honoured guest,
Und trinked de Alle-Spooken peer
  At tinner mit de best.
"Dere ish no Vilfrid Lawson roundt,
  No Andrew Clark I see,
I dinks I shmiles shoost vonce acain,"
  Said Altemann, said he.

Ach! hell erglänzt der Mondschein
  De parrels all amoong
Vhere shtood der Altmann axe in hand
  A-knocking out de boong.
Dey sings de Schvoppingmallartlied,
  Dey hafe a pully shpree,
"Ve ton't care nix for demprance here,"
  Said Altemann, said he.

Dere coomed a debutation
  From de Modern Hishdory School,
Und dell'd him lods of quesdions
  On de soobyect of Home Rule.
"Dere's no man knows shoost vot id means,
  Egceptin' only me,
Und I ton't quite oondershtand meinselbst,"
  Said Altemann, said he.

He vent brofessor's legdurcs,
De brofessors shtay away,
Mitvhiles he hear de Tutorbund
Dot legdures efery day.
" Brofessors gct six hoonderd pounds,
A tutor gets boot dree.
Id 's petter to brofcss ash do,"
Said Altemann, said he.

He vent bolidigal meedins
Vhere de Freiheitgesellschaft rail,
De shbeaker vas an Irishman
Shoost bardoned out of jail.
He hobed dot py de Borduguese
Dis landt gesmasht vouldt pe;
" Dot ish de union of hearts,"
Said Altemann, said he.

He vent von bleasant afdernoons
To valk along de rifer,
De eighds vas here—de eighds vas dere,
Und captains coached forefer.
" Py shinks, vot dime dose vellers keep!
Py tam, how shtill dey pe!
I vish mein barty tid the same,"
Said Altemann, said he.

He shtayed aroundt a vortnight,
  Und dere he shtill might pe,
Boot he saw de crate Brofessor of
  Bolidigal Helodry.
" Gottsdonnerkreuzschockschwerenoth !
  He cooms to dalk mit me,
Dot leds dis ding gombletely out,"
  Said Altemann, said he.

He vent avay a-wafing his
  Oomprella in his handt,
A-vorking his life's mission oudt
  Soobyectifly und grandt.
Soom beoblesh runs de Golfenkunst,
  Soom vorks philologie ;
" I blays de Grandtoldmännerspiel,"
  Said Altemann, said he.

                              S. T

WHAT MIGHT HAVE BEEN!

On October 24, 1892, the Premier delivered in the Sheldonian a brilliant lecture on Mediaeval Universities, and especially Oxford in the time of the Schoolmen. It was currently reported that his colleagues in the Cabinet had experienced of late the greatest difficulty in distracting his attention to any of the questions in home and foreign politics which were pressing for solution.

THEY talk of their Bills and their Ireland, and
    I tell them to go away!
They speak of Uganda and Egypt, but I don't
    hear half they say.
Why should I bother with H-rc-rt, or a nineteenth
    century scene?
Salamanca, Bologna, Salerno! what might—ah!
    what *might* have been!

I'm all for the Schools and the Schoolmen! for
    the battle of word and phrase,
For the grandiose disputation, and the fog of the
    ancient days!
From Naples to Paris I'd triumphed, a Champion
    Churchman I,
Over thirteenth-century L-bbies, *advocatos Diaboli.*

"The Nature of Universals," "the Real and the
    Nominal"—fool
That ever I gave up myself to Eight Hours
    Bills and Home Rule!
When I heckled that Deputation [1]—you remember?
    —six months ago,
Could the *Doctor Subtilis* himself have done
    better? Not *he*, no, no!

How the black-robed crowds had applauded as
    my argument coiled and grew,
Till what in the world my meaning not even my
    own self knew!
Not three, but a hundred courses I'd pointed in
    that or in this,
And been known to all time as the *Doctor
    Perinexplicabilis* !"

D. G. H.

[1] *A certain Deputation from the Unemployed. The Premier treated
it according to his own definition of a Deputation as—" a noun of
multitude signifying many but not signifying much."*

NOCTURNE (1893)

IN the cool and fragrant night,
  When the dews are softly shed,
And the moon is shining bright
  Overhead,—
Only sound to stir the hush is Philomela, o'er
  and o'er
Trilling, trilling in the bushes Her familiar reper-
  toire:
    Nothing else is to be heard
      Save the *cavatine* trite
    Of that overrated bird
      In the night.

As the evening's growing late
  There are acclamations loud
Where the orators orate
  To the crowd,—

And the gentlemen and ladies In the steamy,
    stuffy hall,
Find it quite as hot as Hades As they're jammed
    against the wall,
        While, the speaker's voice submerging,
          Rises still the frequent shout,
        'Mid the swaying crowd and surging,
          "Chuck 'em out!"

        I am quite prepared to war
          For my country, as I hope,
        'Gainst the Kaiser, or the Czar,
          Or the Pope:
Should society require it, Most unquestionably I
With a self-denying spirit Could persuade myself
    to die:
        But to choke upon a platform
          Needs devotion more than mine:
        To be done to death in that form
          I decline.

        Through the dark and fragrant night
          Comes a muffled kind of tread
        (While the moon is shining bright,
          As I said),

There's a sound, a sound of drumming, And a
    tramp of many feet,
There are politicians coming Down the dimly
    lighted street,
      With a song dissimilar
        To the nightingale her lay,—
      And I hear it echo far
      'Neath the vespertinal star,
        'Tis the strain of Ta-ra-ra-Boom-de-ay!

                A. G.

BALLAD OF BLUE B.A.s

Air: " Jock o' Hazeldean."

" WHY weep ye in your home, ladye,
   Why weep ye in your home?
I 'll gie ye Firsts in my new Schools,
   An' ye shall ha' Diplom';
      An' ye shall ha' Diplom,' ladye,
        An' comely fees to pay ":
        But aye she loot the tears doun fa'
        Sair greetin' for B.A.

" A stamp o' wax ye shall not lack,
   Nor parchment rich and rare;
Nor arms in front, nor broidered back,
   Nor signatures sae fair;
      That ye 're the foremost of them a'
        Vice-Chancellor shall say ":
        But aye she loot the tears doun fa'
        For love of that B.A.

The House was decked at morning-light,
 The papers glimmered fair;
The Proctors waited a' the night,
 The Bulldogs baith were there;
  They sought in College and in Ha',
   The ladye wadna stay;
  She 's o'er the border and awa'
   To win a Scots M.A.

         Σ.

VIRGINIBUS

YE Somervillian students, Ye ladies of St. Hugh's,
Whose rashness and imprudence Provokes my
warning Muse,
Receive not with impatience, But calmly, as you
should,
These simple observations—I make them for your
good.

Why seek for mere diplomas And commonplace
degrees,
When now—unfettered roamers—You study what
you please,—
While Man in like conditions Is forced to stick
like gum
Unto the requisitions Of a *curriculum*?

As far o'er field and fallow In flood-time spreads
the Cher,
So wide (yet not so shallow) Your ample studies
are;

As Cherwell's wave returning Flows from a scantier
    source,
So Man's restricted learning Is narrowed to a
    Course.

As when the sphere is fleeting Across th' extended
    net,
And Somerville's competing With Lady Margaret,
As players at lawn tennis Return alternate balls,
E'en such the lot of men is Who read for Greats
    and Smalls!

We bid them try—poor suitors—Yet still to fail
    condemn :
Examiners and tutors Make shuttlecocks of them :
Would you, as some of them are, Be constantly
    betwixt
The horns of a dilemma Uncomfortably fixt ?

When Proctors fine and gate you, If walking
    thro' the town
In pupillari statu Without a cap and gown :
When gauds that now delight you Away you
    have to throw,
And sadly go *vestitu In academico :*

When your untried impatience Is tested every
    day
By rules and regulations : When academic sway
Your study's sphere belittles, You 'll find that life,
    I fear,
Is not completely skittles, Nor altogether beer.

What boots that countless letters Unto your name
    you add ?
And strive to gild the fetters That cramp the
    undergrad ?
Doomed to a course that's narrow Your reck-
    lessness you 'll rue :
The toad beneath a harrow Will happier be than
    you !

A. G.

TO A. G.

A retort from the Ladies' Colleges.

YOU *horrid* A. G.! You unnatural man!
   I don't like your verses *a bit*;
Our JUST ASPIRATIONS you ruthlessly ban,
   And this, Sir, you fancy is wit!

I'm sure you are cross, morose—yes, and *old*,
   If to vote for our hoods you refuse;
I'm positive too you would not be so cold
   If you dropped in to tea at St. Hugh's.

I had an idea for my Bachelor Frock,
   Tailor-cut—not too full in the skirt—
Which has brightened my study of Hume and of
         Locke,
   But *you* think I'm fit only to flirt.

I had carefully planned, when I got the M.A.—
   For *I* don't think the B.A.'s enough—
Not like you poor men, to throw old hoods
         away,
   But to trim such a dote of a muff.

TO A. G.

I scorn your contempt, and disdain your advice;
  I don't see your logical *ergo* ;
And though I could be most uncommonly nice,
  I am now most *indignantly*
                              VIRGO.
                                    B.

IN THE GARDEN

Commemoration after the Battle of the B.A. had been lost.

SHE.

So! you 've remembered! Come, for half an hour,
  Here where the cedar's shadows fleck the green,
Man, monarch Man, monopolist of power,
  Watch how the Woman dominates the scene!

HE.

Yes! what a lesson! *You* with such dominion,
  You beg diplomas, sue for a degree!
Lift but a finger, Man becomes your minion,
  Cringing, confessing *Vicistis Dominae!*

SHE.

Here, yes! we win: but what 's the worth of
    winning
Always the one game from a willing foe,
Gaining no jot on Eve at the beginning,
  Merely because our Maker made us so?

F

HE.

Stop! not so fast! You'd recreate creation,
   Tossing up heads you win and tails we lose,
Claiming in all our rights participation,
   Keeping no less your Empire? We refuse!

SHE.

Empire! what Empire? Look! that pair of
      gabies,
   Mark how his boots shift, see his fingers twitch.
She? there's an Empress! veriest of babies!
   Lord! with how little wit one can bewitch!

HE.

He? you don't know! In Europe at this hour
   No town so hidden but it knows his name.
Power to wield o'er those that have the power—
   Is that not Empire, quintessence of Fame?

SHE.

Bah! who would have it? Give me, give the
      pitied
   Sex, I am born to, a decade's equal chance—
Subtler of speech, light handed, quicker witted—
   Ten years! I warrant *you* 'll not lead the dance!

HE.

Dance? that reminds me! Keep me six and seven.
If you 've an extra to-night—Ah! stand as now!
"Great Herè's angry eyes" in highest heaven
Never flashed queenlier than those, I vow!

SHE.

Sir!! and you 're *laughing?* Know our Cause is
    stronger
Than *you* and such as *you*. We *will* be heard!
Dance o'er the slumbering fires a little longer—
Jack!! you 're not *going?* Don't be so absurd!

D. G. H.

ATALANTA

ATALANTA'S swift and sure,
Atalanta would secure
    A scholarship.
Atalanta's rather "blue,"
And to fame she speeds, 'tis true,
    With hop and skip.

Atalanta's heart is light,
Still the future grows more bright
    With every day:
Atalanta hurries on,
Now another race is won,
    She takes B.A.!

Atalanta, this is bliss!
Atalanta, after this
    For much we look;
Will you teach true wisdom's ways?
Fools from depths of folly raise?
    Or write a book?

Atalanta, here we wait,
Well we know your powers are great,
      Pray what comes next?
Strange! Unwonted! Now we find
Atalanta lags behind!
      We stand perplexed.

Atalanta! Would you fail?
Atalanta! Why so pale?
      Explain it, please.
Atalanta smiles and sighs,
Atalanta low replies,
      " *Hippomenes!* "

THE LATEST APPEAL

After the war of words and pamphlets provoked by the " Women's Degree" proposal.

Vox auditur flebilis atque clamor tristis
"viri docti, parcite! satis effecistis:
enecamur chartulis; temperetur istis
lucubrationibus diu quas scripsistis!"

ex quo primum coeperat muliebre bellum,
sive sit Responsio, sive sit Flagellum
aliquem quotidie iaciunt libellum
Gardner, Anson, Bellamy, Grose, Macan, et Pelham.

tot insignes homines tanta cum scripsissent,
propter haec si ceteri loqui destitissent
Sanctae Theologiae Scholam cum adissent—
certe tamen aliquid scripta profecissent:

sed Magistros ante se videns assidere
nemo tum facundiam potest cohibere,
quin exsurgant invicem, eademque fere
eloquendo repetant ante quae scripsere!

atqui sumus homines constitutae mentis,
nec movemur temere doctrinarum ventis:
iustus et propositi tenax non sescentis
cuiuscumque generis paret documentis.

magni viri, parcite! iam scripsistis satis:
taedet eloquentiae perpetuitatis:
comburendo chartas nos valde fatigatis:
ipsi quin comburitis antequam mittatis?

A. G.

THE INFANT SCHOLAR

What Intercollegiate Competition is coming to. Respectfully dedicated to Trinity College, Cambridge.

IT was a College Tutor who resided by the
    Cam :
    With a pocketful of dollars
    He went out to purchase Scholars,
And he came upon an Infant who was riding in
    a pram.

Said the Tutor to the Infant (and the nursemaid
    stopped the pram),
    "Can you say your A B C ?
    Are you good at Rule of Three ? "
Said the Infant to the Tutor, " Most undoubtedly
    I am."

" In that case," said the Tutor, " I 'm empowered
    for to state
    That the College will supply you
    With a sum—in short, will buy you,
If you 'll patronize that College as an under-
    graduate ;

" And of course we shall expect you, as a simple
   quid pro quo
   (Latin Prose and Latin Verse
   You can study with your nurse),
In your Little-go and Tripos some proficiency
   to show."

" Oh! glorious things are Colleges with money
   to disburse!
   I'm a Scholar—but I *think*,"
   Said the Infant with a wink,
" That I see myself a-doing Latin Prose and
   Latin Verse!"

So this promising young student, having got
   a Scholarship,
   Went completely "on the scoop"
   With his marbles and his hoop,
Neglected quite his alphabet—in fact, became
   a Rip;

And when he came to Cambridge, in his very
   first exam.,
   Disappointing 'twas to find
   The condition of his mind
Was not at all suggestive of ignition of the Cam.

He was wholly inaccessible to study and to cram,
    And he showed no kind of con-
        sideration for the Don
Who had bought him with a Scholarship when
    riding in a pram;

He could not pass his Little-go: he seldom
    wore a gown:
    Drained the far too festive pewter
    Quite regardless of his Tutor:
Till the College wouldn't stand it, and they took
    and sent him down.

There's a moral to this story for the Isis and
    the Cam—
    (Which the motive of these rhymes
    You'll discover in the *Times*):
    'Tis to teach you to be prudent
    In the purchase of a student
That I tell you of the Tutor and the Infant in
    a pram.

                          A. G.

PRAIS OF OXINFURDE

I.

OXINFURDE, thou art *A per se*,
In Art Logyke especiall;
Of Bretane burghis thou beiris the gre,
Be virtewis hyperbolicall:
In thee the lemand lychtis all
Ar gatherit of the sageis cleir;
Thy craft is kene and curiall,
Thy Law is luifly for to leir.

II.

Thy musike and thy mistery
Of dulce poetis rethoricall,
With plesand stevin singand on hie,
Ar blasit throu the warld ouiral:
Thy maisteris philologicall,
Illuminat persounis singulere,
Rehersis verbis potentiall:
Thy Law is luifly for to leir.

III.

Besyd thy watteris flowand fre,
Thy pinnaclis brycht as beriall
Conteinis treasouris of grit deinte
That langis to science ethicall;
Likwys the methaphysicall,
That wes contemnit mony a yeir,
Is buskit into Baliall:
Thy Law is luifly for to leir.

Some tynis their patrimoniall
At cairtis, at gowff, and wantoun geir,
With brokin bainis at the futball:
Thy Law is luifly for to leir.

Quod W. P. K.

AD GERMANOS

YE Germans, whose daring conjectures,
　　Whose questionings darkly abstruse,
Provide our Professors with lectures,
　　Our Dons with original views,
I strive to express what we owe you
　　With wholly inadequate pen :
Too late and too little we know you,
　　Remarkable men !

Had you lived but two thousand years sooner
　　Poor Plato had ne'er been perplexed,
No frequent and fatal *lacuna*
　　Had marred a Thucydides' text:
E'en Pindar would need no explainer,
　　And ne'er had the public misled,
Had he asked a Professor from Jena
　　To write him instead.

Though the facts that you foist on historians
　　To the regions of fancy belong,
And your dreams of the dates of the Dorians
　　Are often demonstrably wrong,—

Though your best emendations be " putid "
When viewed through a critical lens,
Your axioms completely confuted
By grammar and sense,—

Yet O ! till the Pedagogues' Diet
(Determined distinctly to speak)
Prohibits with terrible fiat
The teaching of Latin and Greek,
Till then we will humbly respect your
Contempt for the Probably True,
And climb to the heights of Conjecture
Great Germans, with you !

A. G.

TRUTH AT LAST

LITERARY compositions (thus I heard a Tutor say)
Have, as mediums of instruction, altogether had
    their day :
Be not like our rude forefathers, who their pupils'
    minds perplexed
With their futile speculations on the meaning of
    the text.

In their critical editions we completely fail to trace
That contempt of ancient authors which is Learning's
    surest base ;
Any lies of any writers—Homer, Plutarch, Livy,
    Dem-
-osthenes or Aristotle—all were good enough for
    them.

Mere exactitude linguistic simply serves to hide
    the truth :
Grammar's but a dull convention meant to vex the
    soul of youth :
If you want to Make an Epoch, as a scholar ought
    to do,
Try the methods advocated in the *Classical Review*.

There they teach how quite misleading is Thucy-
    dides' narration
—Save perhaps when illustrated by a recent ex-
    cavation,—
Prove Herodotus a liar—show conclusively that one
Square half-inch of ancient potsherd's worth the
    whole of Xenophon.

If you should consult the classics (and at times
    I think you must,
Just to show they're persons whom it's quite
    impossible to trust),
Do not seek the verbal meaning and the literal
    sense to render:
Read them (like the late Macaulay) "with your feet
    upon the fender."

This be then your chief endeavour,—not to con-
    strue, parse, or scan,
Not to have the least conception what the aorist
    means with ἄν—
But by study of the relics disinterred in various
    spots
Pans Arcadian to distinguish clearly from Corin-
    thian pots:

Thus the purest stream of knowledge from the
    fountainhead you 'll sip :
Thus you 'll do a genuine service to the cause of
    Scholarship :
For by Fact and not by language now the ancient
    world we view—
Which was what our rude forefathers altogether
    failed to do.

                  A. G.

LINES ON MONTEZUMA

BY A PASSMAN.

*An inspiration which he found it impossible to utilize for the
Newdigate.*

MONTEZUMA
Met a puma
Coming through the rye;
Montezuma
Made the puma
Into apple-pie.

Invitation
To the nation
Every one to come.
Montezuma
And the puma
Give a kettle-drum.

Acceptation
Of the nation,
One and all invited.
Montezuma
And the puma
Equally delighted.

Preparation,
Ostentation,
Dresses rich prepared :
Feathers—jewels—
Work in crewels—
No expense is spared.

Congregation
Of the nation
Round the palace wall
Awful rumour
That the puma
Won't be served to all.

Deputation
From the nation,
Audience they gain.
" What's this rumour?
Montezuma,
If you please, explain."

Montezuma
(Playful humour
Very well sustained)
Answers " Pie-dish,
As it's my dish,
Is for me retained."

Exclamation !
Indignation !
Feeling running high.
Montezuma
Joins the puma
In the apple-pie.

D. F. A.

A BANQUET HALL DESERTED

The undergraduate members of a certain College refused to dine in Hall, alleging that the refreshment provided was only good enough for Dons.

PRAESIDENS et Socii laetis cum convivis
epulantur dapibus plane tempestivis:
sed carentes epulis, fame cruciati,
errant in quadrangulis undergraduati.

Compellavi iuvenes, et rogavi "Quare
dira vos inedia vultis enecare?
cur in Aula solus vir assidente nullo
unus secum vescitur, similis Lucullo?"

Dixit quidam pallidus vixque valens loqui,
"crimen est in carnibus quas ministrant coqui.
assuefactus cenae sum delicatiori:
cruditatem metuo, fame malo mori.

Dura iactat ilia fatigatus messor,
multo duriora sunt iactat quae Professor.
quidvis possunt edere Praelectores docti:
nobis cibi displicent nisi bene cocti."

Respondebam puero: "Vera si fateris,
quin placentes epulas aliunde quaeris?
nonne sunt in oppido variae popinae,
Mitre, Grid, et Clarendon, necnon et Reginae?"

"Eheu!" dixit juvenis "admones nequiquam:
nostra clausast janua, nec patebit cuiquam.
graves nobis Socii minitantur poenas
nisi statutorias consumamus cenas!"

.   .   .   .

Praesidens et Socii more vespertino
post finitas epulas oblectantur vino:
verum anteposita fame cruditati
universi pereunt undergraduati.

A. G.

TO HIS PIPE, IN ABSENCE

FAITHFUL companion of my wanderings
By river, road, and mountain : quickener
Of contemplation : comrade, who with me
Hast seen on Alpine pinnacles the dawn
Rubescent, and in lucubration late
Outwatched Orion : fare thee well, my Pipe—
Neglectfully beside the dusty road
Abandoned ! where the weary wayfarer
Halting, from Chiltern's beech-immantled height
Sees through a waving tracery of leaves
The misty plain Oxonian : there thou liest . . .
Blame not thy heedless master : rather blame
The star and black malevolence of Fate
Which all that day hung o'er me, till at eve
Some jagged flint my swift-revolving tire,
Transpiercing, crippled : yet e'en that mishap
I bore more lightly than the loss of thee.
Perchance some tramp thy black but comely form
Hath ravished, and among his beery mates
Exhibits in a wayside public-house

A godsend : where thy sad reluctant maw,
Thy sheeny bowl wherein I took delight,
With horrid shag or villainous returns
He gorges—all unworthy of his prize,
And knowing not the academic care
Wherewith thou once wert tended : now, alas !
Remembering oft thy comfortable home
And studious lair 'mid miscellaneous books,
Thou must associate with common clays,
Old broken clays, and beastly pots of beer.
　Perish the thought ! but with the advancing
　　　spring
May thickening grass and fronds of spreading fern
Protect thee from the spoiler : till perchance
Returning thither on a luckier day
I find thee 'neath the covert, and restore
Thy interrupted honours : once again
To deck my room, a patriarch of pipes.

　　　　　　　　　　　　A. G.

AFTERNOON SERMONS AT ST. MARY'S

"If you attempt to abolish the afternoon University sermons, you will deprive the country clergy of a great privilege, to which they look forward for years, and which is often their sole inducement for keeping their name on the books of their College or Hall."— See Proceedings in Congregation, T. T., 1890.

I.

" RING, men of Pedlington, your chimes uproarious,
Our parson can't and shan't and won't refuse :
He 's had his call to Oxford ; that *is* glorious
    News ! "

" Yes, it came just six weeks ago last Monday,
And I am ready, with discourse and text,
To meet the University on Sunday
    Next.

" I feel how very serious the affair is—
A safety-valve for all my long research—
As I shall show, when preaching in St. Mary's
    Church.

"Long have I waited : now I am invited—
  The proudest moment in my patient life—
So grand for me and my still more delighted
                    Wife !

" My kind Churchwarden puts a pious wish up
  That great Lord Salisbury be there that day.
' Parson is certain to be made a bishop—
                    Eh ?

" ' Yes, certain sure ; if he be rightly treated,
  I don't mind betting you my bottom " bronze,"
Won't he show up those godless self-conceited
                    Dons !

" ' Those unbelieving chaps will, sure, regret it,
  When he cuts up all their new-fangled rot ;
And them there modern heretics will get it
                    Hot ! '

" Good man ! so loyal in fine or stormy weather !
  Who 's known the best and worst of me so
      long !
Perhaps his estimate 's not altogether
                    Wrong !

II.

" I shall speak out *dilucide et plane,*
    With argument and protest, that will make
Professor Driver and Professor Cheyne
                    Quake !

" My words shall keep each master and each doctor,
    And the Vice-Chancellor, from wonted sleep.
I almost think I see the Senior Proctor
                    Weep !

" I see the seats below too full for kneeling,
    And the long galleries which rise behind
With undergraduates from floor to ceiling
                    Lined.

" For this great day I have stored up my know-
        ledge,
    And learned the preacher's most persuasive looks,
For this I kept my name upon the College
                    Books.

" Alas ! too late I grasp the situation,
    And face a truth decidedly unpleasant.
In point of fact there is no congregation
                    Present.

"Like nightmare echoes of unearthly laughter,
    My voice rings through—'as noises in a swoon'—
The vast Sahara of a Sunday after-
                                    Noon.

"By the stove-grating I can see the stoker;
    There's Craddock in the aisle; and, in the rear,
The Bedel sits, who brought me with his 'poker'
                                    Here.

"This is a Pro-Vice-Chancellor; and this is
    A brace of glum Pro-Proctors; and three lean,
Uneasy Freshmen; and the verger, Mrs.
                                    Green.

"Two private friends; a solitary master;
    And in the pulpit, clad in robes and bands,
A very disappointed village pastor
                                    Stands.

"I never could have dreamed that I was fated
    To take my part in such a scene of shame!
I shall remove my unappreciated
                                    Name."

                                    W. W. M.

UBIQUE ?

I TURNED me from the street, opprest
  By uncongenial din,
To where a college promised rest
  Its peaceful shades within :
And there I saw a bicyclist
  Who rode with ardour mad,
With many a skilful turn and twist
  Around (great Heavens !) the Quad.

Ye holders of collegiate posts
  (I cried, and fled away)
Whose ancient venerable ghosts
  Still haunt these cloisters gray,—
Shades of the academic great !
  Behold, how change has wrought
With spots that once were consecrate
  To philosophic thought !

Ye rulers of an earlier race,
  Who, duly capped and gowned,
Would gravely tread with sober pace
  This plot of garden ground,
Till, full of years and college port,
  You laid your gouty bones
To rest beneath your life's resort—
  Your old monastic stones,—

Within your haunts serenely still
  No "scorcher" dared to scorch,
No Blues the midnight cup to fill
  And light the midnight torch:
But we, who other laws obey,
  Scarce blame th' accustomed sight
When cycle wheels profane the day
  And catherine-wheels the night!

Let devious Dons adown the High
  Their course erratic steer,
Let cycle-shops assail the eye
  And cycling shop the ear,
While Scholars, Bachelors of Arts,
  Professors, Proctors, Deans
Still prate about the several parts
  Composing their machines:

Let Tutors, to their tasks at morn
  Accustomed once to trudge,
With lightning swiftness now be borne
  By Singer or by Rudge:
Let Granta's sons the ardour rash
  Or fate malign deplore
Which prostrate laid with awful crash
  Their own Vice-Chancellor:

Still let the tyro's loved resort
  Thy road, O Mansfield, be,
Where Anabaptists watch the sport
  With undissembled glee:
Let Fashion wheresoe'er she lists
  Indulge her latest fads,
But O! from casual bicyclists
  Protect our college quads!

                              A. G.

NORTH, EAST, SOUTH, AND WEST

(AFTER R. K.)

OH! I have been North, and I have been South,
    and the East hath seen me pass,
And the West hath cradled me on her breast, that
    is circled round with brass,
And the world hath laugh'd at me, and I have
    laugh'd at the world alone,
With a loud hee-haw till my hard-work'd jaw is
    stiff as a dead man's bone!

Oh! I have been up and I have been down and
    over the sounding sea,
And the sea-birds cried as they dropp'd and died
    at the terrible sight of me,
For my head was bound with a star, and crown'd
    with the fire of utmost hell,
And I made this song with a brazen tongue and
    a more than fiendish yell:

"Oh! curse you all, for the sake of men who
    have liv'd and died for spite,
And be doubly curst for the dark ye make
    where there ought to be but light,

And be trebly curst by the deadly spell of a
woman's lasting hate,—
And drop ye down to the mouth of hell who
would climb to the Golden Gate!"

Then the world grew green and grim and grey
at the horrible noise I made,
And held up its hands in a pious way when I
call'd a spade a spade ;
But I cared no whit for the blame of it, and nothing
at all for its praise,
And the whole consign'd with a tranquil mind to
a sempiternal blaze!

All this have I sped, and have brought me back
to work at the set of sun,
And I set my seal to the thoughts I feel in the
twilight one by one,
For I speak but sooth in the name of Truth when
I write such things as these ;
   .   .   .   .
And the whole I send to a critical friend who is
learnèd in Kiplingese!

H. A. M.

H

A MEDITATION ON METRE

O IS'T not hard that every bard
   Who seeks to shine in letters
Must still be bound by rules of sound
   And simply dance in fetters?
Would we had lived in ancient times,
   When genius found expansion,
When no one had to hunt for rhymes
   Nor mind the laws of scansion!

They did not go to public schools
   To learn to make a poem,
Nor knew their Quantitative Rules
   As we've been taught to know 'em:
Because—despite what scholars write
   And pedantry rehearses—
Reflection shows that Pindar's prose,
   And only looks like verses.

Yet still from slips in ancient song
  We frame consistent uses,
And when they make their lines too long
  We call it Anacrusis:
When Sappho strays from Reason's ways,
  With reverence still we treat her,
Although she pens what is not sense
  And really can't be metre.

Whene'er some celebrated man
  The critic's ear perplexes
By writing lines that will not scan,
  'Tis Hypercatalexis,—
Should you or I this method try
  To mould our scansion after,
'Twould move, one fears, our friends to tears,
  And stir our foes to laughter!

And so, when Afric's darkest States
  Attain their culture's crowning,
And dusky students read for Greats
  Their Tennyson and Browning,—
Whene'er the critic finds a flaw
  Which now our work disfigures,
He'll make that flaw a general law
  For young poetic niggers!   A. G.

"*VERBERIBUS ET TORMENTIS QUAESTIONEM HABUIT*"

(*Cic. pro Mil.*)

Lines suggested by the repeated heckling of Bodley's Librarian in the assemblies of the University.

INCUSATUS et rogatus
  Ab inquisitoribus,
Tendit manus Bodleianus
  Bibliothecarius.

Circumstantem et minantem
  Turbam supplex adspicit,
Quippe eum culpae reum
  Exsecrandae arguit.

" Effudisti ; pepercisti ;
  Erras, quidquid feceris :
Abnuendo, co-emendo
  Pariter culpabilis.

Scriniorum et librorum
  Usitatum ordinem
Conturbasti et mutasti
  Haud secundum Indicem.

Vultu tristi neglexisti
  Cellas, mensas, forulos,
Atramentum, aestus, ventum,
  Scamna, chartas, calamos.

Et tuorum puerorum
  Manus conducticiae
En! tenellos in libellos
  Causa sunt iniuriae.

Intra fores, Curatores
  Nunquam fere congregant :
Nimis rari vel ignari
  Ut consessum faciant."

·   ·   ·   ·

Nihil horum nobis morum
  Placet, Academici.
Inquinatus est senatus,
  Rixa fit dedecori.
Si superbis subest verbis
  Captiosa actio,
Non est bonum, quaestionum
  Uti artificio.
Reprobatur Alma Mater,
  Sordet Convocatio.

DATE OBOLVM BIBLIOTHECARIO

"Oxford's Poverty: a Letter to the Editor of The Daily News *of Oct. 6, 1894, by Edward W. B. Nicholson, M.A., Bodley's Librarian. Reprinted. Oxford and London: James Parker & Co. Price Twopence."*

EGO custos Bodleianus,
Sicut olim dux Romanus,
Tendo mendicantes manus.

Cives, cives, audiatis
Questum meum paupertatis,
(Quem emisi paene gratis).

Istam exuatis mentem
Quae me fingit affluentem,
Auro superincumbentem.

Vitio Collegiorum
Sum pauperrimus bonorum
Bibliothecariorum.

Squalet domus, sordet tectum,
Saxi opus imperfectum,
Vetustate iam deiectum.

Indices inordinati,
Libri tegmine nudati,
Nummi non dinumerati.

Tabulata forulorum
(Tanta caritas servorum)
Lustra sunt araneorum.

Quod si statum improbatis
Miserandae paupertatis
Huius Universitatis,

Surgant novi Maecenates,
Lautos inter optimates
Nostras merituri grates.

Quod dum fiat, me clamantem,
Me audite supplicantem,
Date pauperi quadrantem.

W. W. M.

EXTENSION IN PARTIBUS

" The University Extension is going to be exhibited as a working model in 1893 at the World's Fair."—Common Report.

THERE'S a hindrance, a check, an embargo
  On all that the student would learn:
For Learning has gone to Chicago
  (Quite possibly not to return):
And many a maid must lament her
  Instructor is vanished and fled—
He has left his Extensionist Centre
  And lectures to Yankees instead!

Six steamers with specimen students
  All qualified fully to teach
(A chaperone noted for prudence
  Is given her passage in each):
While Men, whose agreeable manner
  Accords with their graces of mind—
In fact, who of Culture the van are—
  Will come, in a tender, behind.

They will teach the intelligent Yankee
    That lectures intended to draw
Should roam from ideas of 'Ανάγκη
    To modern conceptions of Law :
We are heirs of dissimilar ages,
    Disjoin or connect them at will,
And pass by the easiest stages
    From Solon and Draco to Mill.

They 'll settle the Aryan races
    Though lost in antiquity dark,
On a proper historical basis
    Establish the date of the Ark :
They 'll prove to the edified nations
    The fact that in less than a week
You may gain (by the aid of translations)
    A competent knowledge of Greek.

They 'll show that you never need fear your
    Researches will weary the brain,
While a person of pleasing exterior
    Is always at hand to explain !
For then, as Experience discloses,
    All teaching of troubles is shorn,
The path of the student is roses
    And wholly devoid of a thorn.

And we, who deprived of their presence
  And all that gives Learning a grace,
Must plod through our usual lessons
  With dull and methodical pace,—
We will greet them with tempered elation,
  Or bear it—as well as we may—
Should the yearning American Nation
  Persuade the Extension to stay!

                        A. G.

A HUMBLE REMONSTRANCE

*" If his (a bonfire) be a provocation, it is one which every citizen is
bound to endure."*—(PROFESSOR DICEY, *in the* Times.)

SIR,—

I am a Unionist, and in any momentous description
    of crisis

It is my invariable custom to read the *Times*, in
    order to see what my leaders' advice is.

(Please excuse my somewhat irregular metre, but
    I find that metre is a thing which is calculated
    the expression of feeling to hinder,

And venture therefore on the present occasion to
    allow myself a certain latitude, on the system
    suggested by Pindar.)

This, as I have said, is my invariable custom in
    any important political crisis,

And I need hardly observe that no counsel is ever
    more valuable than Professor Dicey's :

Still, I should be sincerely grateful to the *Magazine*
    if it would be kind enough to inform its
    numerous readers

Whether the following is a subject on which we
  are bound to be guided by the exhortations of
  our eminent leaders.
Professor Dicey asserts, that in any part of Her
  Majesty's ample dominions
Any person has a right to make any demonstration
  to celebrate the triumph of any opinions :
He says that your opponents, even if they don't feel
  called upon to get drunk and to cheer with you,
Will be acting in a manner not merely wrong but
  also imprudent if they dare to at all interfere
  with you :
And, in fact, that for an Undergraduate to ignite
  a maroon or a bonfire
Is a perfectly legitimate act, which should never
  the indignation of any intelligent Don fire.
It amounts to this : that although a bonfire is what
  I and a number of other persons as an exhibi-
  tion egregious of folly rate,
" If (! ! !) it's a provocation, it is one which every
  citizen " (I suppose a Dean *is* a citizen, after
  all) " is bound to endure and to tolerate,"—
So, the next time that any one celebrates a triumph
  by burning the College, or burning myself,
  I shall still have to bear it, I

Presume,—on pain of infringing his rights as a
citizen,—in a spirit of Christian charity !

Sir, I should like to point out to the Professor, of
course with the proper apologies

For contradicting an eminent man, that what is
right in Belfast is incapable of application to
the interior organization of Colleges :

And I also sincerely trust that if the House of
Lords should reject the Home Rule Bill, as
I understand they 're expected to,

He will accomplish the celebration of his well-
deserved triumph in some place where there is
least likelihood of its being objected to.

There can be no possible difficulty about his
making a bonfire or igniting any number of
squibs, crackers, maroons, rockets, Roman
candles, and Catharine wheels in the decent
obscurity of his proper back garden,

But Professor Dicey himself will acknowledge that
the selection of All Souls College as a scene
for the practical application of his remarks
would be a most shocking example to the
Bible Clerks, and would also in all probability
earn a reproof from the Warden.

A. G.

A BALLADE OF ETHICS

Λέγωμεν οὖν ἀρξάμενοι.

GREY Stagyrite, whom curious time
   Hath sealed each age truth's truer friend,
Since mortal thoughts, when most sublime,
   To thy Academy ascend,
How doth thy ripest wisdom end,
   As ballade with a mad *envoy*?
Who can thy closing rede defend
   Λέγωμεν οὖν ἀρξάμενοι?

Keen Greek, who breathed earth's breath at prime,
   Who hewed the road all thought must wend,
Thy children of a colder clime
   See deeper than thy words intend;
A master's message dost thou send
   To brains, that systems old employ:
" Come let us from our heights descend:
   Λέγωμεν οὖν ἀρξάμενοι."

Here is a scroll for finished rime,
　For balèd wares that merchants vend,
For delvèd glebe, for vaunted mime,
　Yea—for devoutest sighs that rend
Man's heart : say ye, whose backs do bend
　'Neath weight of public grief and joy,
Ere right is done, and manners mend :
　" Λέγωμεν οὖν ἀρξάμενοι."

L'ENVOY.

Sage, since our life all shades doth blend,
　The want unfilled, the promise coy,
We cry the more we comprehend
　" Λέγωμεν οὖν ἀρξάμενοι."

W. J. F.

WINTER

WHILE Cumnor's hill was crowned with snow,
   And winter's icy gripe
Congealed the necessary flow
   Of each domestic pipe,—
When niveous loads with candid weight
   Depressed the silvan bough,
And skaters roamed where pastured late
   The meditative cow,—

I marked, upon a College stair,
   A solitary man,
Who darkly scanned a portal where
   This proclamation ran:
" No lecture will be given to-day:
   The Dean regrets to state
Engagements summon him away "—
   In fact, he's gone to skate.

I passed to Convocation's doors
  With lonely steps and sad,
Where legislators come by scores
  Whene'er the weather's bad :
No object met my vacant gaze
  But benches grim and bare :
No Doctors high, no proud M.A.s—
  Because they were not there !

" And has," I asked, "the slothful Don
  Forgot those sixty-three
Amendments to the Statute on
  The new Research Degree ?
Where is the R-g-str-r," I cried,
  "The Proctors, and the Vice ? "
And Echo mournfully replied
  " They're all upon the ice ! "

A. G.

LINES WRITTEN IN DEJECTION

By an Undergraduate Poet

WHERE'ER I go, whate'er I see,
   I seldom fail to seek and find
Some look, some tone, that feeds in me
   The sadness of the cultured mind.
In weary moods, that please me best,
   I feel like one who wanders down
A misty autumn garden, drest
   In watery green and faded brown.

And when I take my lute and sing,
   How simply sad the numbers flow,
Languorously meandering
   Through quaint cacophonies of woe!
But still one impulse proves me true
   To hearts of less unworldly mould;
My heart leaps up whene'er I view
   The simple pleasures of the old.

I have an aunt of fifty odd,
  Who chirps and chatters like a bird;
Her beaming face, her happy nod,
  Are quite too charmingly absurd.
She finds delight in nonsense rhymes,
  'In Toots, and Gamp, and Swiveller—
Weird shows of mirth!—and yet sometimes
  I wish that I could laugh like her.

When Christmas calls them to be gay,
  My aged kinsfolk all convene;
With them I feast, with them I play,
  Silent amid the bustling scene.
They "turn to mirth all things of earth,"
  They pass their annual jest on me;
They crown the bowl; my pensive soul
  Floats on the current of their glee.

Not all in vain the changing moon
  Strives onward in the vacuous blue;
Not all in vain the rose of June
  Shall drop her gem-wrought veil of dew.
Soon the chill wisdom of the Schools
  On us too shall relax its hold;
And when "life's fitful fever" cools
  We shall be happy, being old.   T. R.

I 2

"READING"

Master.

SCHOLAR, thy books were all untouched to-day,
   The night, no candle in thy rooms was burning:
I fear thou treadest sluggishly the way
   That leads to learning.

Scholar.

Master, the sun is shining in the skies,
   My books, forgive me, how can I be heeding?
Upon the woods the autumn glory lies—
   Yet I was reading.

Master.

Scholar, above us I can see no sun:
   I see no glory where the leaves are falling:
Scholar, thy reading waits thee to be done;
   The Schools are calling.

Scholar.

Master, a way there is thou hast not guessed ;
All wandering from books is not receding ;
For now I live, leave thou to me the rest—
     I have been reading.

Of Life not Aristotle holds the keys ;
Kant cannot heal the heart that lies a-bleeding ;
Nature hath spread her book beneath the trees—
     I have been reading.

Love walked beside me—prate thou not of books—
One fairer far than any sage was leading
My footsteps, master mine, and in her looks
     I have been reading.

FIN DE SIÈCLE

LIFE is a gift that most of us hold dear:
  I never asked the spiteful gods to grant it;
Held it a bore—in short; and now it's here,
    I do not want it.

Thrust into life, I eat, smoke, drink, and sleep,
  My mind's a blank I seldom care to question;
The only faculty I active keep
    Is my digestion.

Like oyster on his rock, I sit and jest
  At others' dreams of love or fame or pelf,
Discovering but a languid interest
    Even in myself.

An oyster: ah! beneath the quiet sea
  To know no care, no change, no joy, no pain,
The warm salt water gurgling into me
    And out again.

While some in life's old roadside inns at ease
  Sit careless, all unthinking of the score
Mine host chalks up in swift unseen increase
    Behind the door;

Bound like Ixion on life's torture-wheel,
  I whirl inert in pitiless gyration,
Loathing it all; the one desire I feel,
    Annihilation!

J. O'R.

HAPPY NIGHT

As in the dusty lane, to fern or flower
Whose freshness in the noon is dried and dead,
Sweet comes the dark with a full-falling shower,
And again breathes the new-washed, happy head;

So when the thronged world round my spirit hums,
And soils my purer sense, and dims my eyes,
So grateful to my heart the evening comes,
Unburdening its still rain of memories.

Then in the deep and solitary night
I feel the freshness of your absent grace
Sweetening the air, and know again the light
Of your loved presence, musing on your face,
Until I see its image clear and whole
Shining above me, and sleep takes my soul.

R. L. B.

TITANIA

"YON sun red-dipping see!
So sets our sway," said she,
"Yet think of me!"
There in the glooming wood,
Like a child's dream she stood,
Dream only good.
"And oh," she sighed, "those mad midsummer
   nights,
With birds to sing sweet measures, stars for lights,
And joys as many as our fancies' flights;
Yet all alike must go, God wills it so!"

"Yon moon a-waning, see!
So wane my spells," said she,
"Yet think of me!"
There in my dreams, she strayed,
Thro' wood and dew-fresh glade,
Moonlight and shade.

" And oh!" she said, "those nights when I might
    glide
To poets' pillows, and their fancies guide
Out of the paths of human lust and pride!
Now no men's dreams I fill, such is God's will!"

Yet when stars a-shining be,
Lost queen of fantasy!
Soft cometh she,
Rose-tired her golden head,
Starlight about her shed,
Sighs o'er my bed.
For she, fair lady, hath my love, and so
May to my sleep her dainty splendours show,
And when that longer sleep ensues, I know,
Where all the ages meet we two shall greet, at
    God's own feet!

                      C. S. A.

ERASMUS SENEX

" *Quumque schedas epistolarum, quas annis superioribus a diversis amicis acceperat, sigillatim evolveret* [ERASMUS], *novae nescio cuius aeditionis gratia, ac plurimae eorum, qui a rebus humanis excesserant, in manus venirent, subinde aiebat,* ' *Et hic mortuus est,*' *ac tandem,* ' *Nec ego diutius vivere cupio, si* CHRISTO *Domino placeat.*' "—Beati Rhenani Selestadiensis Epistola ad Carolum Caesarem praef. ad Opera Des. ERASMI. (Basileae MDXL.)

I.

OLD letters, yellow as the hand
   That turns you over page by page;
Once hot in haste o'er sea and land
   From the prime spirits of the age
On eager mission were you sent :
   Now cold you lie, but eloquent!
Poor crumpled mandates of the great,
Shrewd reasonings of the buried wise,
   Dear balm of love, keen strokes of hate,
Now but an old man's memories.

II.

See these from Luther—how in this
   Stammered the good monk's reverence:
Yet now an autocrat he is
   Divorced from gentleness and sense,
Who, when he launched on waters dark
Would have Erasmus share his bark,
   And, since Erasmus dare not trust
Such crazy guidance through the shoals,
   He flings his clouds of native dust
To blind the eyes of kindly souls.

III.

See this from Colet, early here
   Pressing our life-work's purpose on—
To make the pure Word's meaning clear
   To simple spirits—he is gone!
So 'mid the glow of papal seals,
And wordy monarch's shrewd appeals
   To help their plots with learnèd praise,
I come upon a richer ore,
   Bright words too true for sinuous days
The honest wit of Thomas More:

IV.

Ah! More—the Heavens have oped to thee
  And thy true faith their portals wide,
As unto martyrs painfully,
  Since we praised folly side by side.
Here Hutton's words of venom flow
—Here runs the love of Capnio
  In streams obscure—and neither now
May stir slow monks to wrath again,
  No more hot head or learned brow
Shall sow the truth or harvest pain.

V.

Dead—Colet—More! so many dead!
  The graceful wit, the learning fine;
As o'er their words I bow my head,
  Their souls seem beckoning to mine
To join them, where the scholars meet
At Socrates' and Plato's feet.
  The world, how empty is it grown
Of face of friend and face of foe!
  They leave me on the scene alone—
Surely 'tis time for me to go!

VI.

To leave the stage, where I was brought
    For some wise end that's half-fulfilled
In patient years of toil and thought,
    Half lost by that I wrongly willed—
That end—God's end—was it to hold
The balance fair 'twixt new and old,
    To stablish all the best in each,
Denying each her baseless claim,
    And still the ancient faith to teach,
Purged of the lies and craft and shame?

VII.

Was it to sow good learning's seed
    Unseared by dull scholastic din,
And trust what is God's Word indeed
    To work as He works—from within—
Not, not to leave the future age
A cold dogmatic heritage—
    For sure those years with grander powers
Such close-linked fetters would defy—
    Say! say! lived to plant the flowers
Whose roots live, when the blossoms die.

VIII.

May men hope nothing? whence our haste
　To build Perfection in a day?
Were it not prodigal to waste
　The ordered past? to do away
The Temples where the martyrs knelt,
The holy pages that they spelt?
　They tell me that the court's defiled,
On loathly things they bid me gaze;
　But I have loved it from a child,
And yearn to cleanse it, not to raze.

IX.

Nay—let it stand, as stand it will,
　And let fair Learning's spirit rise,
And Faith's large aisles with incense fill
　To lift men's hearts, and clear their eyes:
And all we give her shall she spread
Eternally when we are dead—
　Till some great day, when down will fall
From temple courts self-purified,
　From ancient arch and mouldering wall
The superstition and the pride.

X.

I knew it—scholarlike the while
　At text and comment, making clear
His Word, I felt a Father's smile
　That said He saw my labour here,
Lost in the vastness of an end
To which both Faith and Knowledge tend—
　No petty gibe of formal spite,
No ecstasies of wild Reform
　At fault could quench that inner light—
I knew my beacon thro' the storm.

XI.

And His, not theirs the voice will be
　That shall arouse me, when I wake,
Who as He had a place for me
　Here in His earth, shall surely take
My spirit to the spirit-home
Of Paul and Plato and Jerome,
　Soon—soon—but not too soon the day:
This spirit's fragile tenement
　By many a toil hath wooed decay,
By many a cureless ill is rent.

XII.

Ah, letters of old dear ones dead,
　　How swift your writers pass away :
And now where spirits bright are led
　　They sup with Cicero to-day !
They clung to life with too slack hold
To have a fear of growing old—
　　Two gifts Athenè gave them—*Life*,
A thing of Light and Grace and Truth.
　　And *Death*—that early stayed the strife
They waged with men—and left them youth.

XIII.

But I have tarried long—beset
　　On either hand with acrid hate
Of bitter minds, whose meshy net
　　Is spread more cunningly of late :
" His work is finished, crafty foes : "
So seem to say yon massy rows
　　From Froben's press, my children all,
That bless me smiling on my face—
　　Basel—not long delays the call—
Give me a quiet resting-place.

W. J. F.

K

IN A MEADOW

THIS is the place
Where far from the unholy populace
The daughter of Philosophy and Sleep
    Her court doth keep,
Sweet Contemplation. To her service bound
    Hover around
The little amiable summer airs,
    Her courtiers.

    The deep black soil
Makes mute her palace-floors with thick trefoil;
The grasses sagely nodding overhead
    Curtain her bed;
And lest the feet of strangers overpass
    Her walls of grass,
Gravely a little river goes his rounds
    To beat the bounds.

—No bustling flood
To make a tumult in her neighbourhood,
But such a stream as knows to go and come
    Discreetly dumb.
Therein are chambers tapestried with weeds
    And screened with reeds;
For roof the waterlily-leaves serene
    Spread tiles of green.

    The sun's large eye
Falls soberly upon me where I lie;
For delicate webs of immaterial haze
    Refine his rays.
The air is full of music none knows what,
    Or half-forgot;
The living echo of dead voices fills
    The unseen hills.

    I hear the song
Of cuckoo answering cuckoo all day long;
And know not if it be my inward sprite
    For my delight
Making remembered poetry appear
    As sound in the ear:
Like a salt savour poignant in the breeze
    From distant seas.

Dreams without sleep,
And sleep too clear for dreaming and too deep;
And Quiet very large and manifold
About me rolled ;
Satiety, that momentary flower,
Stretched to an hour :
These are her gifts which all mankind may use,
And all refuse.

J. S. P.

THE WAY OF THE WIND

E paion sì al vento esser leggieri.

"WHAT do you bring to us, wind blowing in
    from the east,
Sweeping across the Chilterns from far away ?
Oxford has made her ready, prepared the feast,
    Now June's glow is fulfilling the promise of May,
        Now that the nightingales sing;
Herald of health and hope from the rising sun,
        Now that our work is done,
    What is the gift you bear for our week of play,
    Flying with eager wing?"

" Beauty I bring you, and better than beauty, love,
    Love to transfigure your life with its magic
        light :
As in the dawn while stars still shimmer above,
    Wakens the sun to brighten the dark of night.
        Welcome the wonderful thing!

Now it calls you, let not the calling be vain,
    Think not it comes again;
  Swift is the coming hither, more swift the flight
    Hence, of the gift I bring."

"What do you take from us, wind blowing on to
    the night,
  Out by winding river, by field and flat,
Bearing away with no pity the day's delight,
    Leaving the places empty, where late there sat
    All that we loved the best?
Herald of sorrow and sadness, hurrying chill
    Down from the darkening hill,
  Love was ours and beauty, but this and that
    Pass like a careless guest."

"Onward we wander, beauty and love and I,
  Yet we are not lost, we have gone before;
Doth the sun stand still in the orient sky?
  Doth he not speed, as we, to the further shore
    Set in the golden west?
All things follow, why should ye wait behind?
    Follow ye too and find
What was yours, and shall be for evermore,
  There in the land of rest."
                     S. T.

LINES ON AN OLD THEME

As in a dream I heard all humankind
  Singing together: for a whole day long
  Troop caught from troop the antiphon of song
Where none outran and none was left behind.

First rose the song of Youth with the rising sun,
  The slow hours of the morn with music
      winging;
  And Joy was all the burden of his singing,
The Joy of all things to be thought and done.

So Pleasure broadened in the breadth of light,
  A thousand rivers flooding one great sea,
  Until his large diffusion rolling free
Touch'd the eternal verges of delight.

And so Youth pass'd, but with the perfect noon
  Came graver quires of men in life's mid span,
  Who set the latter excellence of man
To a more sober and advisèd tune—

Chanting how action ripening 'neath the eye
  Of him who plann'd, and high hopes full
    achieved
  (Mature strength proving all young faith be-
    lieved)
Made the bud blossom and the fledgeling fly.

These also pass'd as eventide drew near,
  And with twilight appeared a new succession,
  Old men, who sang how peace excels possession,
Age rounds to the full Youth's sunny hemisphere;

How looking back they saw that life was well,
  Nor mourn'd their inactivity who lay
  Sheaves reap'd and garner'd for the threshing
    day.
An hour they sang, then ceas'd, and darkness fell.

                                        J. S. P.

LINES FOR THE PLOUGHMAN
IN HOLBEIN'S "DANCE OF DEATH"

I.

ONE furrow more; and thy bare feet shall rest,
  And thy tired hand be still:
There is thy church upon the low hill's crest,
  And the sun behind the hill.

II.

Set thy dim eyes on these; God brings thee sleep
  Within the toilsome field;
Turn to thy home once more, where they will weep,
  Seeing all thy troubles healed.

III.

God bring thee sleep, but these are very dear,
  Home and the setting sun:
Look on them once again, then have no fear;
  Thy long rest is well won.

A WELCOME

SUMMER again is with us, and, crowning the
    summer, my queen—
Summer for which we waited, and you that
    tarried so long—
Now that the flowers have blossomed, now that
    your beauty is seen,
    Where is our loyal greeting, where is the
    song?

Once there was treasure of singing, once, in the
    golden time—
Ah! the wonderful days that are not, the songs
    that of old we sung!
Careless and quick they came, rhyme hasting to
    mate with rhyme,
    When the strings were fresh for playing, when
    I was young.

Squandered is now the treasure, the rhymes are
    scanty to-day;
    The fingers have lost their cunning, the heart
    of the singer is cold:

How shall I honour my queen, or the excellent
    beauty of May,
      Now that the strings are failing, now I am
      old ?

Nay, but I must, for you will it, bidding me
    welcome again
    Blossom and bird of summer, and one who is
    fairer than all:
Nay, but a song must be sung—since of singing
    my lady is fain—
    I hear and obey her summons, answer her
    call.

Therefore we bid you welcome, fairest of months
    and of maids,
    Now that the frosts of winter have vanished
    and fled away,
Greeting with service of song, and with music of
    flashing blades,
    The coming of her we longed for, the coming
    of May.

                      S. T.

AT LLANSANTFRAED

Henry Vaughan died 1695.

I.

OLD Silurist—thou lov'st the name
Dear to fables, dear to fame—
How slow the heavy years have crept
While Llansantfraed her watch hath kept
Here where thou sleepest lone
Beneath that ancient mossy stone
That still to pitying God doth say
Its 𝔐iserere 𝔊loria.
But no : thou hast not slept, but rather wed
In ripe communion, wit well-seasonèd
With holy Herbert and his gentle peers
Hast joyous hailed the years.

II.

"𝔖erbus inutilis, peccator maximus!"
Are all thy graces reckoned thus?

Nay: here the Angel with glad eye
Big with eternity
Shall light, and knock with friendly hand,
For ever 'mid the Angels didst thou stand,
Passing from care of painful men
Back to the Temple gates again,
Where, through the whirl of chance and time,
Ran over linking rime to rime,
In seasons, dawnings, sunsets, nights and days,
God and His praise.

III.

Poet: who taught thee so to strain
Those healthful draughts for pain
That with them still we cozen death
Drinking God's mountain-breath,
Stored in thy curious simples from the hills
Of native Brecon, while our ills
We lose, assured that earth for all her gloom
Is Heaven's ante-room ;
Where heralds wait, and sure anticipations
And prophecies of new creations,
And old loves glorified?
So surely wert thou fittest guide

To him, who truly-born interpreter
Of Nature's voice as thou, revered in her
God's emblem—yea, and looked behind
With the same longing of his wistful mind
On shadowy glories brought from otherwhere,
That children with them bear.

IV.

Poet-physician—thou didst see
Heaven in earth, in man eternity:
Thy "watery wealth" of cataracts
Leapt from God's lake, thy upland tracts
Reached to the bounds of Paradise,
Where two worlds mated for thine eyes
Both near to thee, though one be far,
Beneath one morning-star:
No sunshine-ray, no April shower
But fed thy placid spirit's flower;
No mountain blossom didst thou press,
But spake to thee of holiness—
I ween that thou, whose earthly eye
Saw Heaven so nigh,
There seest things of mortal birth
Clear as was Heaven to thee on earth,

And better lov'st in that celestial air
Sights that e'en here were fair?
Still binding in sweet union
God's Heaven and earth in one.

V.

For us in earth and air sound on
The myriad voices' mingled tone:
But who can read as thou that unknown tongue,
Or tell us what is sung?
Who brings again our apathy to melt
The spirit-sculpture of the Celt?
Ah! yet 'neath Nature's pomp the soul he knew
The constant vision still is true,
And there man's soul made clear and bright
Greets its own features with delight,
As wondering truth all-new in water lies
For down-gazing childish eyes.

W. J. F.

"*LES BELLES ROSES SANS MERCIE*"

A. D. 1460.

" O pity, pity, gentle heaven, pity!
  .   .   .   .
Wither one rose, and let the other flourish!
If you contend, a thousand lives must wither!"
     KING HENRY VI, PART III, Act ii, Sc. 5.

HEIGH! brother mine, art a-waking or a-sleeping?
Mind'st that merry moon of roses a many sum-
  mers fled?
Mind'st thou the green and the dancing and the
  leaping?
Mind'st thou the haycocks and the moon above
  them creeping?
Mind'st thou how soft were the pillows of our
  heaping?
Mind'st thou our dole when the merry day was
  sped?
I do mind how every night
Thou would'st pull me roses white,
Ancient sign of our proud line, argent rose on
  verdant bough!

Heigh! sweetheart mine, art a-waking or a-sleep-
ing?
Seest again the roses that blossomed long ago?
Seest again the garden with its paths so still and
shady?
Seest again the dew lie as beads for night's white
lady?
Seest thou aught else but the blue eyne of thy
maidie?
Seest thou their brimming in their pity of thy
woe?
Sweet, I see thee offer up
Roses red as wine in cup,
Such befit (thou sayest it) golden head and lily
brow!

Heigh ho! ye twain, that should wake in lieu of
sleeping!
Rue ye that rose-time when the roses all were reft?
Ruest thou, sweet heart, that the favour red thou
worest?
Ruest thou, my brother, that the badge of snow
thou borest?
Rue ye that noon when the fight flashed thro'
the forest?

L

Rue ye the maid's tears so life-long lonely left?
Rose of white, and rose of red,
That did each one claim her dead,
Twining be at amity round about my window
    now !

C. S. A.

TWO LONG VACATIONS

Grasmere.

SEVEN we were, and two are gone:
  Two! What are those remaining?
Ghosts of the Past, with cloud o'ercast,
  Cloud that is always raining!

Ah me! Last year, when I came back,
  Like faithful hound returning
For old sake's sake to each loved track,
  With heart and memory burning;

There was the knoll, there was the road,
  There was our humble dwelling;
There o'er the Raise of Dunmail showed
  The shoulder of Helvellyn;

And there the great heights black with cloud,
  Whence flowed the white stream under;
And glens with echoing torrent loud,
  And cataracts' distant thunder;

L 2

And seven men's eyes looked dimly out
  Beneath our old house rafter;
And seven men's forms crept round about
  With peals of ghostly laughter;
And sad yews dripped on the mossy stone;
  And fuchsia and rose grew rank;
And the woodbine wept as the rain poured on;
  And ferns spread over the bank;

And trees o'ergrown shut out the light
  Of Easedale's cascade falling;
And hearing, after-born of sight,
  No longer heard it calling.

And no one cared: save only there
  Where flowers make silence sweet,
By pilgrims worn, that rocky stair!
  Look up! It is Wordsworth's seat.

Where glassed in those far-reaching eyes
  He read all nature plain;
And saw more things in earth and skies
  Than will ever be seen again.

There found he wealth, to others dearth,
  And peace, from a world's wild din;
And, would we know the soul of earth,
  He bade us look within.

All else is changed. Yet rain may pour,
  Weeds spread, and all grow rotten;
But something lives from days of yore,
  Still fresh, still unforgotten:

The lamp of truth we lit in youth,
  The dreams of life's young morning:
In that dark hour I found their power
  Still in the embers burning.

O vows, I cried, so oft denied,
  And you resolves forsaken,
Befriend me still! A new-born will
  Trusts in you newly taken.

But, how to live, oh, tell me friend,
  In age still wisdom gaining?
The clouds descend; ah, bid them blend
  With fires of youth remaining!

A. G. B.

HORA ADEST

IT is late ; the sun is setting ; it is time for us
    to go :
The shadow-light is creeping down the sky :
There's a melancholy music through the branches
    soft and low
For the passing of the breezes as they die.
But now above, and now below, a passionate
    refrain
Is throbbing to a paean loud and long :
For us the tones and tremors of a melody of
    pain,
For you the chime and cadence of a song.

We have lived ; but you are living : we have
    twisted ropes of sand,
For you the web of tapestry is meet ;
You shall weave the varied blossoms of this
    long-enchanted land
With the tender grass that grew beneath our feet :

And we shall watch, and smile at you, and
   wondering if we
Had half your verve and vigour, shall inquire,
"*If ever to grow older, and to leave it all, could be*
   The course of any decent man's desire?"

Well, we know our days are over: and we really
   wouldn't stay;
Besides—we have an antiquated air:
We simply cannot swagger in the very latest way,
   Nor imitate the fashions that you wear.
Our work is done; and poorly done: but if we
   could begin
And start afresh, and take another load;
The chances are that native ineradicable sin
   Would meet us and upset us on the road.

Meanwhile the cultivation of a captivating smile,
   A *savoir-faire*, a cynical disdain,
Will win us to the world within a very little
   while,
   And bring us all to love of life again:
The world that lives, the world that moves, will
   claim us for its own,
   The ancient order yielding to the new;

And our lips will breathe an ether that would
    warm a heart of stone—
But still we shall not cease to envy *you*.

For when some of us are clerics, and when some
    of us are not;
And when most of us have drifted to the Bar;
When a few of us have ruled the roast in some
    too-torrid spot,
And we absolutely don't know where we are:
A sign—a dream—an echo—from these conse-
    crated towers,
A message, or a murmur, or a breath,
Shall move to life the measure of the fervour
    that was ours,
And must be ours and yours for life or death.

H. A. M.

AN EDITOR'S GOOD-BYE

THE year's two dozen numbers all are past,
  Proofs and Corrections gone beyond recover;
I too must go, yet turn me at the last
  And look things over.

Some there be, so they tell me, who suppose
  An Editor's existence beer and skittles,—
They little know the toil he undergoes
  To earn his victuals.

Some think him happy, sumptuous, witty, bland,
  Oft in the Parks magnificently dining,
While happy damsels sit on either hand
  And watch him shining.

Some think him scornful, donnish, stern, sedate,
  Holding all changes vile as revolutions,
Burning the brilliant undergraduate
  His contributions.

Vain dreams, alas, of happy souls! the Parks
  Receive me coldly in their gilded mansions;
The Undergraduate who in verse embarks,
  Sinks in his scansions.

Thoughts of next number wear me day and night.
   Both ends I burn a saddened lifetime's taper,—
I only wish my critics had to write
   A high-class paper.

   *   *   *   *   *   *

So now farewell to thee, loved *Magazine*,
   Farewell to "notes," to verses and to "leaders,"
Farewell to you who for a year have been
   Long-suffering readers.

J. F. W.

THE END

www.ingramcontent.com/pod-product-compliance
Lightning Source LLC
Chambersburg PA
CBHW020014030726
47500CB00002B/590